The Adventures of Mr Pink-Whistle

The Adventures of Mr Pink-Whistle

Enid Blyton
Pictures by Kevin Kimber

BLOOMSBURY
CHILDREN'S
BOOKS

The Adventures of Mr Pink-Whistle was first published in 1941 Newnes
First Published by Bloomsbury Publishing Plc in 1997
38 Soho Square, London W1V 5DF

Enid Blyton

Copyright © Text Enid Blyton Limited 1941
Copyright © Illustrations Kevin Kimber 1997
Copyright © Cover illustration Ian Inniss 1997

The moral right of the author and illustrator has been asserted
A CIP catalogue record of this book is available from the British Library

ISBN 0 7475 3219 2

Printed in Great Britain by Clays Ltd, St Ives plc

10 9 8 7 6 5 4 3

Cover design by Mandy Sherliker

Contents

Chapter 1

The Little Secret Man

'It isn't fair,' shouted Mr Pink-Whistle, 'it isn't fair!'

He stamped round the room in a rage, and his big black cat looked at him in alarm, and put her tail under her, out of his way.

'Here I've just been reading about a poor man who saved up and bought a nice new teapot for his wife – and on his way home a boy on roller-skates banged into him and broke his precious teapot!'

Mr Pink-Whistle put his hands under the back of his coat, pursed up his lips, and looked at his cat. 'Now is that fair, Sooty?' he shouted. 'Is that fair? Did anybody buy him another teapot? No! And look here – here's a picture of a little girl who ran to pick up

something for a friend, and was knocked
over by a car! Now, I ask you, Sooty – is *that*
fair?'

'No-ee-oh-ee-ow,' answered Sooty in
surprise.

'Well, I don't think it's fair either!' said Mr
Pink-Whistle. 'I do think that if people are
kind, they should be rewarded, not punished
– and what's more, Sooty, I'm going to do
something about it.'

'Oh-ee-ow!' said Sooty, waving her tail a
little.

'Sooty, you know that I'm rather a lonely

little man, don't you?' said Mr Pink-Whistle with a sigh; and he stroked his big black cat, who began to purr at once.

'You see, Sooty, I'm not like ordinary people,' went on the little man, sinking down into a chair. 'I haven't any real friends except you. The reason is that I'm half a brownie and half a proper person – so the brownies don't like me much, and ordinary people are afraid of me because I've got brownie ears and green eyes like you.'

'R-r-r-r-r-r-r,' purred Sooty softly. She knew how kind her master was, even if he was only a half-and-half.

'*But*, Sooty, I've got a secret!' whispered Mr Pink-Whistle into his black cat's pointed ear. 'Yes, I've got a secret that I've never used yet. I can make myself invisible whenever I like!'

Sooty didn't know what Mr Pink-Whistle meant. She stared at him out of eyes as green as her master's.

'I'll show you what I mean, Sooty!' said Mr Pink-Whistle. He shut his eyes and murmured a few strange words that made Sooty tremble and shiver.

And then Mr Pink-Whistle disappeared!

One moment he was there – and the next he was gone. Sooty blinked her eyes and looked all round the little warm kitchen.

Her green eyes nearly fell out of her head in surprise. Where, oh, where had Mr Pink-Whistle gone?

Sooty heard a faint giggle – and there was Mr Pink-Whistle back again! Sooty put her ears back and looked alarmed. 'Mee-ow-ee-ow!' she said. She hoped her master wasn't going to do this sort of thing very often.

'Now, that's my secret,' said Mr Pink-Whistle, pleased. 'And what I'm going to do, Sooty-cat, is to go into the big town and look out for unlucky people. I shall go into their houses, and I shall disappear into thin air, so that they don't know I'm there. And I shall see that they get a reward for being kind! What do you think of that for a good idea, Sooty?'

'Wow-ee-ow,' answered Sooty.

'You'll stay here and keep house for me,' said Mr Pink-Whistle, 'and I'll come back and see you often. Now I'll pack my bag and go. I won't let unfair things happen to people. I won't! I won't! I may be only a half-and-half, but I'll just show the world what I can do!'

He packed his bag, rubbed his face against Sooty's soft head, ran out of the front door, and waved goodbye.

Sooty watched her kind, funny little master go, and wondered what he would do.

'He won't be happy away from his cosy little home,' said Sooty. 'I know he won't. I wonder whose house he will go to?'

Now, in the nearest town lived a hard-working little woman called Mrs Spink. She had four small children, and it was very hard to feed and dress them properly. They didn't have many treats, but they were good little things and didn't grumble.

One day they all came rushing home from school in excitement. There was Teddy, with blue eyes and golden hair; there was Eliza, with red curls; there was Harry, with golden curls; and there was Bonny, with a mop of dark hair like a sweep's brush. They tore into the kitchen and made Mrs Spink jump so much that she almost upset the pan.

'Mother! Mother! There's a party at school on Thursday and we're all to go!' cried Teddy.

'But you haven't got any nice clothes,' said Mrs Spink. 'Not any at all! You've only got the ones you have on.'

'Can't you wash them, Mother, and make them nice and clean?' asked Eliza, almost in tears at the thought of not going to the party. Why, they had never been to one before!

'Well, on Wednesday afternoon you must all go to bed, so that I can wash your clothes ready for the party the next day,' said their mother. 'That is the best I can do for you.'

Teddy, Eliza, Harry, and Bonny were quite willing to spend an afternoon in bed if only their mother would get their clothes ready for the party. Then she could wash them, iron them, and mend them.

So on Wednesday afternoon all the four children undressed, got into their ragged little night-clothes, and cuddled into bed, with books to read. Mrs Spink took the dirty clothes into the garden, set up her wash-tub, and began to wash all the clothes – socks, stockings, vests, knickers, shorts, shirts, petticoats, dresses, jerseys – goodness, what a lot of things there were!

Mrs Spink sang as she worked. She saw a funny little man with big ears and curious green eyes looking at her over the fence as she rubbed and scrubbed.

'Good-day,' he said; 'you sound happy!'

'Well, my four children are going to their first party tomorrow,' said Mrs Spink, squeezing the dirty water from a frock, 'and that's enough to make any mother happy! Poor little things, they don't have many treats. I'm just washing the only clothes they have, so that they can go clean and neat.'

When she looked up again, the funny little man was gone. That was strange, thought Mrs Spink. She hadn't seen him go! She pegged up all the clothes on the line, emptied her tub, and went indoors to get the tea.

And do you know, the line broke, and

down went all the clean clothes into the mud! Would you believe it!

Poor Mrs Spink! When she came out to see how the clothes were getting on, she could have cried. All of them were far dirtier than before!

'Well, well!' said Mrs Spink, in as cheerful a voice as she could manage. 'I'll just have to wash them all again, that's all!'

So she set to work once more, and put all the clothes into her wash-tub again. How she rubbed and scrubbed away! She didn't see the funny little green-eyed man again – but he was there, all the same, watching her. He was sitting on the fence, quite invisible.

'It isn't fair!' he muttered to himself. 'After she washed all those clothes so beautifully! No, it isn't fair!'

Mrs Spink couldn't mend the line. It was so rotten that she was afraid it might break again, so she took all the clean clothes and spread them out flat on the grass at the front of the house to dry. Dresses, petticoats, socks – they were all there, as clean as could be.

Mrs Spink went in to take the kettle off the fire, for she really felt she could do with a cup of tea. Mr Pink-Whistle slipped in behind her, though she didn't see him. He sat on a chair, and thought what a nice, clean little kitchen it was.

And then a dreadful thing happened. Two dogs came into the front garden, and what must they do but run all over those nice clean clothes! They didn't miss a single one! So when poor little Mrs Spink went out to get them, there they were all covered with dirty, muddy footmarks.

She didn't cry. She just stood and looked and gave a heavy sigh. But Mr Pink-Whistle cried! The tears rolled down his cheeks, because he was so sorry for Mrs Spink.

'It isn't fair!' he whispered to himself. 'She worked so hard – and it was all for her children. It just isn't fair!'

Mrs Spink gathered up all the clothes and put them into her wash-tub again. She washed them clean for the third time, and she hung them up on the big airer that swung from the kitchen ceiling. Then she went upstairs to see how the children were getting on.

'I'll have to iron your clothes in the morning,' she told them. 'First, the line fell down and then two dogs ran over the washing. It's all in the kitchen now. Nothing can happen to it there.'

But she was wrong. Something did! A big heap of soot tumbled down the chimney, and when Mr Pink-Whistle looked up at the clothes they were all black with the flying soot!

'How dare you!' cried Mr Pink-Whistle, shaking his fist at the soot. 'How dare you! Oh, I can't bear this! I can't. I must put it right; I must – I must!'

And out he rushed to put things right – funny old Pink-Whistle!

Chapter 2

Mr Pink-Whistle
Puts Things Right

Well, what do you think Mr Pink-Whistle meant to do? He meant to go and buy new clothes for all the four children! Good old Mr Pink-Whistle!

He was so upset to think that the clothes had been spoilt for the third time, after Mrs Spink had worked so hard and so cheerfully, that he had to blow his nose hard to keep from crying.

'It's not fair!' he kept saying. 'Why do these things happen when people try so hard? I won't have it! I shall put it right. It's no good being sorry about things if you don't do something to put them right!'

He quite forgot that he was invisible still, and that people couldn't see him. So, when

17

he walked into a clothes shop and the door-bell rang, the girl there was most alarmed to hear a voice and to see nobody!

'I want to see some party clothes,' said Mr Pink-Whistle. 'For two little boys and two little girls.'

'Oooh!' said the shop girl, frightened, for she could still see nobody. 'There's somebody speaking and there's nobody here! Help! Help!'

'Oh, sorry!' said Mr Pink-Whistle, remembering that he couldn't be seen. At once he came back again, and his fat little body, big ears, and green eyes appeared in front of the surprised girl.

'Now don't run away or do anything silly,' said Mr Pink-Whistle. 'It's a secret I have – I can make myself disappear or not. Please show me the children's clothes you have.'

The girl looked into Mr Pink-Whistle's kind red face, and knew that he couldn't harm anyone. She took down some boxes and drew open some drawers. In a little while she and Mr Pink-Whistle were talking about what would be best for Teddy, Eliza, Harry, and Bonny to wear at the school party.

They chose new vests, warm and white. They chose knickers and socks, two pretty petticoats, two pairs of grey flannel shorts for the boys, and two blue silk frocks for the girls. Mr Pink-Whistle chose a green jersey for Harry and a red one for Teddy.

'Would that be all, do you think?' asked the girl, who was really quite enjoying herself now, for Mr Pink-Whistle had told her all about poor Mrs Spink, and she was feeling quite excited to think of the surprise that this funny little secret man was planning.

'Well – what about hair-ribbons for the two girls to match their frocks?' asked Mr Pink-Whistle. 'Or don't girls wear them now?'

'Oh, of course they do!' said the shop girl, and she measured and cut two fine hair-ribbons of blue silk for Eliza and Bonny. 'Oh, and have the children shoes, sir? Did those get spoilt too?'

'Well, Mrs Spink didn't wash the shoes,' said Mr Pink-Whistle. 'But I remember seeing them in the kitchen – very poor old shoes, too. I'd better have four pairs, I think.'

So they chose brown shoes that they thought would fit the children – and then that was really all. The girl did everything up in a big parcel and gave it to Mr Pink-Whistle. They beamed at one another, pleased to think of the secret they both shared.

Mr Pink-Whistle paid for the things. Then he said goodbye and went. He ran straight back to Mrs Spink's. He nearly forgot to make himself disappear, but just remembered in time. Then he opened the door and marched in, unseen by anyone.

Mrs Spink was still upstairs with her children. She didn't know anything about the sooty clothes downstairs yet. Mr Pink-Whistle looked round the black kitchen and frowned.

'I can't put the children's clothes here,' he thought. 'They would get sooty. What about the next room?'

Now in the next room was a big chest of drawers where Mrs Spink kept all the clothes of the family, and all the sheets and towels. Mr Pink-Whistle tiptoed to it and pulled the drawers open. The top one and the bottom one were empty. So Mr Pink-Whistle carefully and neatly put the boys' clothes into the top drawer and the girls' clothes into the bottom one. They looked lovely. Mr Pink-Whistle felt very happy as he packed them in.

Mrs Spink ran down the stairs to the kitchen. When she saw the sooty clothes and the black kitchen, she gave a cry of horror. And then, because she was so tired, she sat down on a sooty chair and began to weep.

'My beautiful washing!' she wept. 'Oh, I did think nothing more would happen to it! I'm too tired to do it again – but what will the poor children say if they've no clean clothes to wear at the party tomorrow? Oh dear! Oh dear! Things are very hard!'

The children came running down the stairs to see what was the matter with their mother. Mr Pink-Whistle watched them from the other room. Would they be angry? Would they be sulky – or very, very sad?

When they saw what had happened they were full of dismay and horror, for they knew that their poor mother had already washed the clothes three times. They flung their arms around her and hugged her.

'You won't be able to go to the party, my dears!' wept their mother. 'I'm too tired to wash the clothes again.'

'Mother, *we* don't mind!' cried Teddy.

'Mother, it doesn't matter a bit!' cried Eliza.

'Don't you cry, Mother; we'll help you wash again tomorrow,' promised little Bonny.

'We don't mind about the party!' cried Harry, though he did really mind, dreadfully.

'Nice children, kind children!' said tender-hearted Mr Pink-Whistle to himself, feeling for his handkerchief again. 'Oh, I'm glad I'm here to do something! I can't bear things like this to happen!'

'You're the best children in the world!' said their mother, and kissed them all. 'And that's just why you, of all children, should have a treat. It isn't fair!'

'No, it's not!' said Mr Pink-Whistle in a loud whisper. The children heard it, and looked surprised. Mr Pink-Whistle thought it was time that they saw what he had done for them, and he pulled open the top drawer and rattled it a little.

'What's that noise?' said Mrs Spink in surprise. 'I hope the cat isn't in my parlour, messing things up!'

They all went into the little parlour. They didn't see Mr Pink-Whistle of course,

23

because he was invisible, but they bumped into him without knowing it!

'Who has opened this top drawer?' wondered Mrs Spink, catching sight of the half-opened drawer. She went to shut it – and then she stared – and stared – and stared!

'Look!' she said in amazement, and pulled out of the drawer all the new socks, jerseys, vests and shorts belonging to the boys. 'New clothes! And new shoes too! Good gracious! Where did they come from!'

The girls pulled open the other drawers and soon found their new clothes in the bottom drawer. How they squealed and shrieked when they saw their blue frocks and ribbons to match!

In a trice the four children dressed themselves. Mr Pink-Whistle had guessed their sizes exactly. They all looked as sweet as could be, and if Mr Pink-Whistle had been their father he couldn't have felt prouder of them all.

'I don't understand it, I don't understand it!' said Mrs Spink, thinking she must be in a lovely dream.

'Now don't be frightened,' said Mr Pink-Whistle suddenly, 'because I'm going to *appear*. One, two, three – and here I am!'

And there he was! All five looked at him in astonishment. 'Did *you* put those new clothes there?' asked Mrs Spink.

'Yes, I did,' said Mr Pink-Whistle. 'I'm tired of seeing and hearing and reading about things going wrong in this world. I can't bear it! It's not fair! So I'm just taking a little holiday to put some of the things right. And I was so upset about your having to wash those clothes so often that I felt I *must* go and buy some new ones. I do hope you don't mind.'

'You're a darling!' cried Bonny, and she suddenly hugged him. It was the first time Mr Pink-Whistle had ever been hugged and he thought it was lovely.

'Well, this is my first try at putting things right,' he said. 'I'm glad it is a success. Now be sure you enjoy your party tomorrow, my dears!'

'We couldn't help enjoying it, with all these fine clothes!' cried Eliza, dancing round the room in her blue silk. 'Thank you, dear kind little man!'

Mr Pink-Whistle felt so happy that he thought he would burst. He hurriedly muttered the magic words that made him invisible again, and he disappeared. 'Goodbye!' he cried. 'Goodbye! I'll come and see you again sometime. I'm off to find something else to put right. Goodbye!'

'Goodbye!' cried the children, wondering where their peculiar, green-eyed friend had gone. He was off through the falling night, as happy as could be.

'Now for something else!' he said, with a skip and a jump. 'Now for something else!'

And he'll find it all right, as you'll very soon see!

Chapter 3

The Girl with
the Broken Doll

Well, Mr Pink-Whistle's next adventure was with a little girl who had a beautiful new doll. Her name was Jessie, and one day when she passed by the toy shop window, she saw the most lovely baby doll she had ever seen, sitting there looking at her.

The doll was dressed in woolly clothes, and had a round woollen hat on its head with a bobble at the top. Its eyes were wide open and had long lashes. Its mouth smiled, and it had tiny little shining nails on its fingers and toes.

Jessie stood still and looked at the doll for a very long time. She loved it with all her heart. She longed to have it in her arms to

27

hold. She longed to put it to bed in her toy cot.

'How much is that doll, Mummy?' she asked.

'It is very expensive,' said her mother, looking at the ticket on it. 'It is ten pounds. Don't ask me to buy it for you, because I haven't even got one pound to spare!'

'No, I won't ask you, Mummy,' said Jessie. She turned away from the doll, and went home. But all the time she was having tea she remembered the doll's face and how its big brown eyes had looked at her, with their long curling lashes. And when she was in bed that night she remembered the doll again and wished she had it with her to cuddle.

'I shall save up, and save up, and save up till I have ten pounds,' said Jessie to herself. 'Mummy says if you want a thing badly enough you can get it in the end, somehow! So I will get that lovely doll. Its name shall be Rosemary Ann. Sometimes I shall call her Rosemary and sometimes I shall call her Ann!'

Then Jessie began to save up. She saved all her Saturday ten pences. She saved one pound that she had for her birthday. She saved fifty pence that Uncle Fred gave her and twenty pence that Aunt Flo gave her. Every time Mummy gave her ten pence for running an errand or helping, she put that into her money-box too. She didn't spend anything on sweets.

She found twenty pence in the street one day, and as she couldn't find out who had lost it, Mummy let her put that in her money-box too. And at last, after three whole months, she had ten pounds!

'This is the most exciting day of my life,' said Jessie to her mother that morning. 'I am going to buy that new doll for my very own. She is to be called Rosemary Ann. She has such a lovely face, Mummy, and you should just see her dear little finger-nails and toe-nails!'

Jessie got the cot ready for her new doll. She found a doll's cup and saucer for her to drink from. She got ready her doll's pram to fetch Rosemary Ann from the shop. Then she put her ten pounds into her bag and set off happily, thinking joyfully of the lovely doll that would so soon be hers.

There it was, still sitting in the window. Jessie ran inside the door, put down her money, and bought the doll. And at that very moment Mr Pink-Whistle came along, looking for an adventure! He couldn't be seen, for he was quite invisible. He wouldn't let himself be seen in the town if he could help it, because people laughed at his big ears and green eyes.

He saw Jessie's happy face and was pleased. He followed her into the shop without anyone knowing. He saw the little girl buy her doll. He watched her take it into her arms and hold it there lovingly.

'You feel beautiful,' said Jessie to the doll.

'Your name is Rosemary Ann. I saved up for you for three whole months. I didn't buy any sweets. I didn't spend even five pence, because I wanted you so badly. And now, you darling Rosemary, I've got you! You're mine! There's a cosy cot waiting for you at home, and a chair, and a cup and saucer – and there's your pram outside ready to take you home!'

The doll looked up at Jessie out of her big eyes. Jessie pulled the woolly hat straight and hugged Rosemary.

'I'm happier than I've ever been in my life!' she said. Mr Pink-Whistle beamed all over his red face. This was what he liked to hear. So many people were sad or hurt or disappointed, but now here was someone happy. He followed Jessie out of the shop and watched her tuck the doll up carefully in the blue pram. Then Jessie took the handle and began to push the pram proudly home, hoping that people would look into it and see the fine new doll.

But almost at once a dreadful thing happened. A crowd of boys came along with a big dog. They were shouting and laughing, and the dog was very excited. It kept jumping all around the boys and trying to lick their faces.

And just as the boys and the dog reached Jessie, the dog jumped up to one of the boys, fell sideways, and knocked Jessie's little blue pram right over!

Rosemary Ann was jerked out on to her head. There was a loud crack, and Jessie gave a scream.

'Rosemary! Oh, Rosemary's broken!' The little girl picked up her poor doll, and looked in horror at the broken face. The nose was smashed, and the lovely eyes had gone inside Rosemary's head. She was quite, quite spoilt.

'I say! I'm sorry our dog did that!' said one of the boys. 'It was quite an accident. Shall we scold the dog?'

'Oh no,' said poor Jessie, with hot tears trickling down her cheeks. 'Don't scold him. He didn't mean to do it. Oh, I'm so unhappy. I've only just this minute bought Rosemary Ann, and I saved up for three whole months to buy her. And now she's broken, the poor, poor thing!'

'Perhaps your mother will buy you another one,' said a boy.

'I shan't ask her to,' said Jessie, wiping her eyes. 'She hasn't got much money.'

The boys ran off with their dog and soon forgot about Jessie. Mr Pink-Whistle was left, standing invisible beside the pram. He was terribly upset. He sniffed so loudly that Jessie heard him and looked around. But she couldn't see anyone, of course.

Mr Pink-Whistle felt angry and upset and sad and unhappy all at once. He walked round the corner and stamped up and down in a rage. 'It isn't fair! It isn't fair! That's a dear little girl, and she saved up so hard, and did so love the doll, and then the dog came and broke it. Now she's very, very unhappy. And the doll's broken so much that it can't be mended. What am I to do to put it right? It really isn't fair, and I won't have it!'

Suddenly Mr Pink-Whistle knew what to do. He made himself appear suddenly, much to a small boy's surprise, and rushed into the toy shop. He banged on the counter. The shop woman appeared and looked surprised to see a fat little man wiping his green eyes with an enormous yellow handkerchief.

'Have you got another doll like the one the little girl bought just now?' he asked.

'Oh yes, of course,' said the shop woman, and she lifted one out of the box. Mr Pink-Whistle snatched it up, slammed down the money, and tore out. The shop woman really thought he was quite mad.

Jessie was walking home with her pram.

She had put poor broken Rosemary Ann into it again, with her face towards the pillow, so that she couldn't see how broken she was.

Mr Pink-Whistle hurried up, and just as he got near, he dropped two or three pennies. They went rolling all over the place. 'Dear, dear!' said Mr Pink-Whistle, pretending to be vexed. 'Now where have they gone?'

'I'll get them for you,' said Jessie, just as he had known she would. She put her pram by the side of the pavement, and went to pick up the pennies. As quick as lightning Mr Pink-Whistle whipped the broken doll out of the pram and put the new one in, face downwards. He stuffed the broken one into one of his big pockets, and covered up the other doll.

Soon Jessie came up to give him the pennies. 'What's the matter with your doll?' he asked. 'Why do you make her lie face downwards?'

'Because she's broken,' said Jessie, nearly crying again.

'Now, how lucky that is!' said Mr Pink-Whistle. 'I can mend broken dolls! Look! I just tap her on the back of the head gently – like this – and say "Hi-tiddle-hi-to, hi-tiddle-hi-to!" And hey presto! – the doll will be all right again!'

Jessie didn't believe him. She knew dolls weren't mended like that. But to please the funny little man she turned her doll over – and then she gave a scream.

'Rosemary Ann! You *are* all right! Your nose has come back! Your eyes are looking at me! You're quite, quite well! Oh, you darling! I'm so happy!' She snatched the doll out of the pram and hugged it as if she would squeeze it to bits. Mr Pink-Whistle felt all funny about the eyes again, and blew his nose loudly. This was fun! He'd put something right again! Good!

'Thank you ever so much,' said Jessie, her eyes shining with happiness. 'You must be magic!'

'I am, a bit,' said Mr Pink-Whistle, and his big ears waggled like a dog's and his green eyes gleamed. 'Well goodbye, little friend! Don't forget me, will you?'

'Oh, never!' said Jessie. 'I think you're really wonderful!'

So no wonder Mr Pink-Whistle skipped off as if he were treading on air. 'I've done it again! And I'll do it a third time before I'm much older! Yes, I certainly will.'

Chapter 4

A Marvellous Afternoon

Jackie Brown was so excited that he could hardly keep still. He kept hopping about, first on one foot and then on another, till his mother told him to go out into the garden and hop there, on the smooth green grass.

'I shall be a grasshopper then!' said Jackie. 'Oh, Mother, I'm so excited! Tomorrow I'm going to see the conjurer at the flower show. There's a great big tent there, and for twenty pence everyone can go in and see the conjurer. I've got twenty pence and I'm going!'

'You've told me that about twenty times already!' said his mother, laughing. 'Go along out and play, and just think of something else for a change!'

But Jackie couldn't think of anything else. He had seen a conjurer once before, and the magic things he did were so wonderful that the little boy had never forgotten them. Fancy, he even made a rabbit come out of an empty glove! Jackie had known it was empty, because it was his own glove that he had lent to the conjurer!

'And tomorrow the conjurer will do lots more magic!' said the little boy happily. 'Oh, shan't I enjoy it!'

He saw Eileen and Dick next door, and he climbed over the wall to play with them. Dick had a new kite and he was trying to fly it. It was a lovely one.

The wind suddenly took it up very high, and Dick squealed with delight. 'Look at it!' he shouted. 'It's flying like a bird!'

But it didn't fly like a bird for long. The wind dropped and down came the kite – and it fell on top of the greenhouse! Dick tugged it. It was stuck tightly.

'Oh, bother!' he said. 'It's stuck! What shall I do?'

Jackie took the string and pulled gently. It was no use, the kite was held fast by something. 'Wait till the gardener comes, and he'll get a ladder and get it down for you,' he said.

'I did want to fly it this afternoon with Uncle Harry,' said Dick. 'He promised to take me to the hills.'

'Well, perhaps I can get it for you if the ladder isn't too heavy to carry,' said Jackie. He found the ladder, and the three children carried it carefully to the greenhouse. They set it up at the back, and Jackie went up the rungs.

He came to the kite. The string was wound round the spike at the top of the greenhouse. Jackie pulled hard, and then let go of the top of the ladder to undo the string.

The ladder wobbled – the ladder fell! Crash! Jackie and the ladder reached the ground together! Poor Jackie! He banged his head so hard on the ground that for a moment he couldn't get up. He felt peculiar. Then he sat up and held his head.

'You've cut your head on a stone,' said Eileen, frightened. 'It's bleeding. Come and show my mother, quickly.'

It was such a bad cut that Jackie had to have his head carefully bathed and bound up in a bandage. The little boy had had a

bad shock, and his mother called in the
doctor.

'The cut will soon heal,' said kind Doctor
Henry. 'But he must be kept very quiet
indeed for a day or two, Mrs Brown, to get
over the shock. Put him to bed.'

'Oh, I can't go to bed – I can't, I can't!'
wept poor Jackie. 'I want to see the conjurer
tomorrow at the flower show. Oh, please let
me go!'

'I'm afraid you wouldn't enjoy yourself a
bit, if you went all the way to the flower show
and back, with that dreadful aching head of

yours,' said Doctor Henry. 'Be a good boy and lie quietly, and you'll soon be right. The conjurer will come again next year, I expect.'

'But next year is so far away!' wept Jackie, more disappointed than he had ever been in his life before. 'My head feels all right, really it does. Oh, I do want to go and see the conjurer! I'm so unhappy! All I did was to try and help Dick get his kite down – and now I've got a most unfair punishment, because I'm not to have my treat.'

'It's very bad luck, old man,' said the doctor. 'Very bad luck. But these things do sometimes happen, you know.'

'It shouldn't have happened when I was doing somebody a good turn,' wept Jackie.

'No, it shouldn't,' said the doctor. 'You deserved a better reward than this!'

Poor Jackie! He was put to bed and there he had to stay. Dick and Eileen knew all about it next day, and they were very sad indeed. 'Just because he tried to get down my kite!' said Dick gloomily. 'It isn't fair!'

A small fat man, with strange big ears and bright green eyes like a cat's, was passing by when Dick said these words. He stopped at once.

'What isn't fair?' he asked.

Dick told him all about Jackie, and how he had hurt himself doing a kind deed, and now couldn't go to see the marvellous conjurer.

'He's very unhappy about it,' said Eileen. 'We've sent him some books to read, and I've lent him my best jigsaw puzzle – but I'm sure he'll cry all the afternoon when the time comes for the flower show.'

'Too bad, too bad!' said Mr Pink-Whistle – because, as you have guessed, he was the little fat man! 'I can't bear things like this, and I just won't have them. I shall put this right somehow!'

The two children stared in surprise at Mr Pink-Whistle. There was something very strange about him – and in a minute there was something even stranger still, because he just simply wasn't there! He had vanished before their very eyes!

'Where's he gone?' said Eileen in great surprise.

You would be surprised to know where he had gone! He had crept up to a rabbit-hole in the field nearby and had made a noise like a juicy carrot. Up came a tiny fat baby rabbit – and Mr Pink-Whistle caught it and put it into his pocket. Then he went back to Jackie's house. Nobody could see him, of course.

He climbed up a pipe and looked in at a window.

In the bedroom there was a small boy lying in bed with his head bandaged up, and tears rolling down his white cheeks. It was Jackie, feeling very unhappy because it was the afternoon of the flower show and he couldn't go to see the conjurer.

Mr Pink-Whistle sighed. He hated to see anyone unhappy. He climbed quietly in at the window and stood looking at Jackie.

'Hello!' he said suddenly.

'Hello!' said Jackie in surprise, looking all round to see where the voice came from. There wasn't anyone he could see at all.

'I'm a conjurer, come to do a few tricks for you,' said Mr Pink-Whistle.

'Good gracious!' said Jackie astonished. 'But where are you! I can't see you!'

'Well, you see, I'm so magic that I'm invisible at present,' said Mr Pink-Whistle. 'Now just tell me a few things you'd like to hop from the mantelpiece on to your bed, and they'll come!'

Jackie giggled. It was funny to think of things hopping from the mantelpiece to his bed. 'I'd like the clock to come,' he said. At once the clock seemed to jump from the mantelpiece and land on Jackie's bed! Of course, it was really Mr Pink-Whistle carrying it, but, as Jackie couldn't see him, it looked as if the clock came by itself!

Then a china pig flew through the air and back again. The coal-shuttle did a little jigging dance round the room, all by itself –

though, of course, it was really Mr Pink-Whistle carrying it and jigging it about. But it did look so very funny!

Then Jackie's teddy bear stood on the rail at the foot of his bed and danced a comical dance, sticking his legs out just as if he were doing steps! Jackie laughed till he cried. He couldn't see Mr Pink-Whistle's hands holding the bear. He thought the bear really was doing it!

'Now ask any of your toys to speak to you, and hear them talk!' cried Mr Pink-Whistle, thoroughly enjoying himself. It was so lovely to make somebody happy.

'Well – I'd like my old toy soldier in that corner to say something to me,' said Jackie, sitting up in bed.

Mr Pink-Whistle, quite unseen, walked to where the soldier was sitting. He made it wave its hand to Jackie, and then he talked for it, in a sort of gruff voice.

'Hello, Jackie! Get better soon!'

'Oh, Soldier! I never knew you could talk before!' cried Jackie, very excited. 'Horsey, can you talk to me too?'

His old horse stood in the corner. Mr Pink-Whistle made it jiggle about, and then he spoke for it. 'Nay-hay-hay-hay-ay! Nay-hay-hay-hay-ay! Hurry up and get better and ride on me, Jackie! Nay-hay-hay-hay-ay!'

Jackie was thrilled. 'You've got a lovely, neighing voice, Horsey!' he said. 'Oh, what fun this is! How magic you are, Mr Conjurer!'

'Pink-Whistle is my name,' said Mr Pink-Whistle politely. 'I'm glad you like the magic I do.'

'I only wish you could make a rabbit come out of somewhere, like the other conjurer did,' sighed Jackie. 'That was really most surprising magic.'

Mr Pink-Whistle felt the little baby rabbit in his pocket, and he was delighted that he had thought of bringing it.

'Where would you like the rabbit to come from?' he asked.

'Oh, out of my bed!' said Jackie. 'It would be lovely to have a rabbit in bed with me! And Mr Pink-Whistle, couldn't I see you please? You sound the kindest, nicest person I've ever heard.'

'Do I really?' said Mr Pink-Whistle, feeling very happy. 'I'm glad. Well – you *shall* see me, Jackie. Just look at the clock on the mantelpiece for one whole minute, and at the end of it, look at the foot of your bed. I'll be there!'

Now whilst Jackie was busily watching the clock, waiting till a minute had gone by, Mr Pink-Whistle carefully and quickly put the tiny rabbit into Jackie's bed, at the foot. Then he said the words that made him appear, and just as Jackie had counted the whole minute, there was Mr Pink-Whistle grinning away at him at the foot of the bed, his green eyes shining brightly.

'Oh! How nice and funny and jolly you are!' cried Jackie – and then he gave a squeal, because something was creeping up his bed. He put his hand down – and pulled out a baby rabbit!

'You're more magic than the other conjurer!' shouted Jackie. 'You really are! You're – you're . . .'

And just then the door opened and Jackie's mother came in to see what the

noise was. Mr Pink-Whistle disappeared just in time.

'Look! Look! A conjurer has been here, and he made this rabbit come out of my bed!' squealed Jackie. 'Oh, I'm so happy! It's my very own rabbit for me!'

'But there's no conjurer here!' said Jackie's mother in astonishment, looking all round. And yet – the rabbit was certainly there. How very, very strange!

A little giggle came from the window, out of which Mr Pink-Whistle was quietly climbing. Down he went – and off into the world again to find something else to put right. Hurry, Mr Pink-Whistle!

Chapter 5

The Dog Who Lost his Collars

Now once Mr Pink-Whistle had a rather peculiar adventure. It was with a little terrier dog.

The dog's name was Jinky, and it lived with its master and mistress in a nice little house in the town. Jinky was a friendly dog, and loved to welcome people, and he was always ready to put out his small red tongue to lick anyone.

But now, week after week, he was in disgrace. His mistress and master scolded him hard. It was the first time, and he was very unhappy.

'You are a very bad little dog to keep losing your nice new collars!' his mistress said to him. 'You lost your first new red collar, and we bought you a green one with your name on it. You lost that the very next day! Then you had a fine brown one with bright studs all round it – and you came home without it the next week! And now you have lost the new blue one we gave you yesterday!'

'Woof!' said Jinky sadly.

'You are very naughty not to want to wear your collar,' said his master sternly. 'All dogs wear collars. So do their masters! You should be proud to be like your master! I can't imagine how you get your collar off, you bad dog – but just remember this, that you will be scolded and locked up in your kennel every time you do it!'

Jinky's master banged the kennel gate and left poor Jinky shut up inside. He was very sad. He lay and whined pitifully. It wasn't fair! He hadn't lost his collars! A horrid big boy had taken them away from him each time! But he couldn't tell his master that, because he could only talk doggy language, and no two-legged people understood it.

Just then somebody came by who *did* understand whines and yelps and barks. It was fat little Mr Pink-Whistle of course! He was half a brownie, and his big pointed ears could understand all that the birds and animals said, just as the real brownies could.

So Mr Pink-Whistle could hear all that poor Jinky was saying as he passed by the little house. To you and to me it might have sounded like 'Ooooo! Oooooo! Oooooo! Yelp, yelp, yelp! Oooooo! Oooooo!'

But to Mr Pink-Whistle it sounded like this:

'Oh, how sad I am! Oh, how unfair everything is! Oh, what a poor little dog I am, scolded for nothing! Oh, and how I love my master and mistress, and now I have made them very unhappy; but I couldn't help it, and they have made *me* unhappy too – but they *could* help it! Oh, tails and whiskers, I wish I wasn't a dog!'

Mr Pink-Whistle stopped and listened in astonishment. What could be the matter with the poor little dog? He made himself disappear and then he walked up the garden path and looked for the kennel. Inside was Jinky, his head on his paws, whining away to himself.

'What's the matter?' asked Mr Pink-Whistle in surprise. Jinky looked up. He couldn't see anyone, but he could smell somebody. How peculiar!

'It's all right,' said Mr Pink-Whistle, patting Jinky. 'I'm here, though you can't see me! Tell me, what's the matter?'

So Jinky told him his trouble. 'I'm being punished for something I didn't do,' he whined. 'But my master doesn't understand me when I try to tell him. A nasty, horrid boy keeps putting down lovely bones in the next street, and when I go to smell the bone, the boy pops out and catches me. Then he takes off my collar, and sends me home without it.'

'Well, what a wicked thing to do!' said Mr Pink-Whistle, very angry. 'And you've been scolded for that! Poor little dog, it's a shame! It's not fair! I must put it right.'

He undid the kennel gate and Jinky slipped out of his kennel and out of the yard into the garden. 'Now you come along with me,' said Mr Pink-Whistle. 'We'll go and find this boy. Keep at my heels. You can smell them, even if you can't see them! We'll do to that boy a little of what he has done to you.'

Together they trotted down the street and round the corner. People meeting them only saw a small dog with a new collar round his neck – but Mr Pink-Whistle was there all right too! But he couldn't be seen.

'Look!' said the dog, stopping. 'There's a lovely bone over there. I'm sure it's put there by that boy, so that I or any other dog shall go to it. Then he would catch us and steal our collars.'

'Well, you run up to it and smell it,' said Mr Pink-Whistle. 'Don't be afraid. I shall be near you.'

So Jinky ran up to the bone – and close beside him was Mr Pink-Whistle. As soon as Jinky reached the bone and sniffed at it, a big arm came over the fence and caught hold of the little dog. He was pulled right over the fence – and there behind the fence was a big boy with a horrid sly face.

'Another collar!' he grinned. But he didn't grin long! No – something most extraordinary happened!

Something took hold of him and wrenched at *his* collar! Something pulled at his tie. Something jerked at his coat – and before he could do anything to stop it, his collar, tie, and coat were taken right off him.

'Don't! What is it? Who is it? I can't see anyone!' cried the frightened boy. 'Go away! Go away!'

'I'm only doing to you what you've done to little dogs!' said a stern voice in his ear. 'Off with your shirt! Off with your boots! Off with your socks!'

Off came everything except the boy's vest and trousers!

'Next time you think of stealing anything, just think of Mr Pink-Whistle!' hissed a voice in his ear. 'Yes – Mr Pink-Whistle! I'll come after you again and take your clothes away if you dare to steal another collar from a dog!'

'Mr P-p-p-p-pink-Whistle, please give me b-b-b-b-ack my clothes!' wept the boy. 'My

mother will scold me if I go home without them.'

'Good!' said Mr Pink-Whistle. 'Very good. Go home and get scolded then!'

And the angry little man pushed the naughty boy so that he almost fell on to his nose. He ran off, howling and crying, wondering fearfully who Mr Pink-Whistle was. He couldn't see him – but he was there all right!

Mr Pink-Whistle went to the nearest dustbin and stuffed the clothes in without being seen by anyone. Jinky licked his hand, after smelling about it for some time. The little dog thought Mr Pink-Whistle was wonderful.

'Now you go home, too,' said the fat little man, patting Jinky kindly. 'And don't be afraid of that boy any more. He's not likely to worry you or any other little dog again!'

Then off went Jinky very merrily, his tail in the air. Off went Mr Pink-Whistle too – and you may be sure that if he had had a tail it would have been straight up in the air as well, just like Jinky's!

Chapter 6

A Surprise For Dame Gentle

There was once an old woman called Dame Gentle, and she was just like her name. She was a dear old thing, and all the children loved her.

She was very poor, and sometimes, like Mother Hubbard, when she went to the cupboard – the cupboard was bare!

One day she had a bit of luck. Mrs Biddle wanted some scrubbing done, and she asked Dame Gentle if she thought she could do it.

'Of course!' said Dame Gentle. 'Haven't I rubbed and scrubbed all my life? A good bit of hard work never hurt anybody! I'll come along tomorrow and do whatever you want me to. Ah, I'm pleased about this, Mrs Biddle. I want a new blanket for my bed, and a new kettle for my stove. Maybe I'll be able to get them now!'

Well, she worked very hard indeed, and when the cleaning was done she had enough money to get what she wanted. She was very happy.

'Now for once I'll give myself a real treat!' said Old Dame Gentle. 'It's my birthday next week, and I'll make myself a cake, and get in a tin of cocoa to make some hot cocoa. I'll boil the water in my new kettle, and I'll be warm at night under my new blanket. Ah, I'm in luck's way just now!'

She asked Mother Dilly to come and share the cake and the cocoa with her, for she was a generous old thing. When the day came, Dame Gentle ran out to ask one of her neighbours for a few flowers to put on her table.

And whilst she was gone, who should come to the open door but Mister Mean! He rapped. Nobody answered. He pushed open the door a bit wider and looked inside. Dame Gentle was not there!

Then Mister Mean saw the new cake on the table, the tin of cocoa, and the new blanket set out ready to show Mother Dilly when she came. His mean little eyes gleamed with delight. He tiptoed into the kitchen, put the cake and the cocoa into his pockets, and rolled up the nice new blanket. He threw it over his shoulder and ran out of the room and down the path.

Just in time too – for Dame Gentle was coming back with a few flowers for the table. She trotted up the path to the front door, which she had left open, and walked into her warm kitchen.

'Mother Dilly will be here in a minute,' she thought. 'I wonder if that kettle's boiling.'

And then she saw that her beautiful new cake was gone! And the tin of cocoa! And the lovely warm blanket!

Dame Gentle stared as if she couldn't believe her eyes. *Where* had they gone to? She looked all round. She looked in the cupboard – but the cupboard was bare!

'Somebody's stolen them!' she said, and she sank down into her chair. 'Oh, how mean! To steal from an old, old woman like me! My lovely cake – and my beautiful blanket – all gone! What a horrid thing to happen on my birthday!'

There was a knock at the door and Mother Dilly walked in. 'What's the matter?' she cried, when she saw how sad Dame Gentle looked.

'Somebody has stolen all my birthday things, that I worked so hard to get,' said Dame Gentle, wiping her eyes. 'It's upset me a bit.'

'What a shame!' said Mother Dilly, putting her arms round her friend. 'Oh, what a shame! Who stole them?'

'I don't know,' said Dame Gentle. 'I just ran out to get those flowers, and when I came back everything was gone – even the tin of cocoa!'

'Now don't you cry, dear,' said her friend. 'I'll just run home and get a bit of tea, and two pieces of shortbread that I've got left in my tin. And we'll eat those for your birthday.'

She left the old woman and hurried out into the street, really angry to think that someone should have treated old Dame Gentle so badly. She bumped into a fat little man with curious green eyes, as she ran out of the gate.

'Oh, I beg your pardon!' said Mother Dilly. 'I'm feeling rather hot and angry, and I didn't look where I was going.'

'Hot and angry!' said Mr Pink-Whistle in surprise, for of course it was the little secret man who happened to be passing by. 'What's the matter?'

'Somebody has taken the cake, the cocoa, and the new blanket that my poor old friend, Dame Gentle, worked so hard to get,' said Mother Dilly fiercely. 'Isn't it a shame?'

'It certainly *is*!' said Mr Pink-Whistle,

pricking up his ears at once. 'Is she a kind old soul?'

'The kindest in the world!' said Mother Dilly. 'She doesn't deserve such bad luck. I'm sure it's that horrid Mister Mean who has done this. He is such a sly creature, and not at all honest.'

'Really?' said Mr Pink-Whistle. 'Where does he live?'

'He lives at Cherry Cottage, round the corner,' said Mother Dilly. The little fat man raised his hat and ran off. Mother Dilly wondered who he was and what he was going to do.

Mr Pink-Whistle made himself disappear when he turned the corner. Then quite invisible, he looked for Cherry Cottage. Ah – there it was, at the end. He walked quietly up the path and looked in at the window.

Mister Mean was there, grinning away to himself. He had got the cake on the table, and had already eaten half of it. He had made himself a fine jug of hot cocoa from the cocoa powder in the tin, and he had draped the new blanket round himself to see how warm it was.

So of course Mr Pink-Whistle knew at once

that Mister Mean was the thief. 'The mean, hateful creature!' he said to himself. 'Making an old woman unhappy, just when she had got a little treat ready. Ah, well, Mister Mean, you'll be sorry.'

Mr Pink-Whistle walked up to the door, gave it a loud crack with his fist and flung it open. He stamped in and made a sort of angry growling noise in his throat.

'Who's that?' cried Mister Mean in alarm, for he could see nobody, of course.

Mr Pink-Whistle said nothing. He just made the angry growling noise again. He went to the larder door and threw it open. It was full of goodies! There was a meat pie, a jam tart, a tin of biscuits, two kippers, a large tin of best tea, and some tins of meat. There was a big white loaf of bread in the bin and a pound of butter on a plate.

'Good!' Mr Pink-Whistle growled in his throat. 'Very good! I'll have those!'

He began to take them all off the shelves. Mister Mean, who was shivering in his shoes, jumped up at once. 'Stop thief!' he cried. 'Stop thief! Those are my belongings!'

Mr Pink-Whistle growled again. 'I'm only doing what you've just done this morning!'

he said. 'Where did you get that cake from? Where did you get that blanket? You wicked fellow, to rob an old woman!'

Mister Mean was so terrified to hear a voice and not see anyone that he fell down on his knees and begged for mercy.

'Mercy!' shouted Mr Pink-Whistle, who was now beginning to enjoy himself. 'No! You shan't have any mercy. I might even eat you up!'

'Oh no, don't, don't!' begged Mister Mean, who at once thought that Mr Pink-Whistle must be an invisible giant or something. He didn't know that he was a little man much smaller than he, Mister Mean, was! 'Take all you want – but leave my house and don't come back again. You frighten me! I can't see you! I'll never steal again, never, never, never!'

'Well, see you don't,' said Mr Pink-Whistle, 'or I shall certainly come back and gobble you up in one mouthful!'

Mr Pink-Whistle could hardly keep from giggling when he thought how difficult it would be for him to gobble up Mister Mean. He took the new blanket, and a new rug from the sofa, and set off to Dame Gentle's, carrying as well all the goodies he had found in the larder.

Mother Dilly hadn't yet come back. Dame Gentle had gone into the bedroom to wash her face. There was no one in the kitchen.

Mr Pink-Whistle draped the blanket over one chair and the rug over the other. He put the meat pie, the jam tart, the biscuits, kippers, tea, bread and tins of meat on the table. Then, hearing footsteps, he slipped quietly to one side, and waited.

Dame Gentle came into the kitchen at the same time as Mother Dilly came back. They both saw all the new things at the same time. How they stared! They rubbed their eyes and stared again.

'Do you see what I see?' asked Dame Gentle at last. 'Goodies of all kinds! *And* my blanket and a new rug as well!'

'I see it all!' said Mother Dilly. 'It's very strange – but very pleasant. Let's sit down and eat!'

'Oh, I'm so happy again,' said Dame Gentle. 'Somebody was *very* unkind to me – but now someone else has been even kinder! Blessings on him, whoever he may be! Blessings on his kind head!'

'Thank you,' whispered Mr Pink-Whistle, longing to show himself, but not daring to, in case he frightened the two old ladies. 'Thank you!'

'Funny!' said Dame Gentle, looking all round. 'I thought I heard something. IS ANYBODY HERE?'

But nobody answered. Mr Pink-Whistle had slipped out of the door, and was already on the way to his next adventure. Kind old Pink-Whistle!

Chapter 7

The Two Ugly Creatures

There was once a man that nobody loved. He lived alone in a cottage, and he was angry because he was blind.

He wore black glasses over his two blind eyes, and the children did not like these. So they were afraid of him, and the rudest of them called names after him, which was very unkind of them.

The man had always had weak eyes, but he had been so fond of reading that he had made them worse and worse. Now he couldn't see at all, and he was unhappy and angry. Angry because he knew that if only he had been wise, he would still have been able to see – and unhappy because he wanted to read, and couldn't, and because he had no friends.

People would have liked to be kind to him, but he wouldn't let them. He was bad-tempered, spiteful, and very, very lonely. His face grew uglier and uglier as he frowned more and more, and his black glasses seemed even blacker.

He used to go along the road of the town, tapping with his stick, and muttering to himself as he went, 'It isn't fair. I haven't anything at all! I've no friends. I've no books to read, no pictures to see. It isn't fair!'

And one day, of course, fat little Mr Pink-Whistle met him and heard him. What, something wasn't fair? Ah, Mr Pink-Whistle was all ears when he heard that, you may be sure.

'What isn't fair?' asked Mr Pink-Whistle, falling into step with the blind man.

'Go away,' said the blind man rudely. 'I never talk to anyone. Go away.'

'Then you must be very lonely,' said Mr Pink-Whistle in his gentlest voice.

'What's that to do with you?' said the blind man. 'I'm ugly, I know – even the children call out after me, the little wretches. And I'm bad-tempered. And I'm quite helpless, because I can't see. I often fall off the kerb

into the road – but who cares? Nobody at all!'

'You are a very unhappy man,' said Mr Pink-Whistle with a sigh. 'I wish I could find you a friend. All you want is someone to love, and someone who loves *you*.'

The blind man laughed loudly. 'Who would ever love *me*?' he cried. 'If anyone sees me, they run away. I know. I've heard them!'

'Let me help you across the road,' said Mr Pink-Whistle, his heart very sad, for he could not for the life of him think how he might put things right for this poor man.

The blind man at first pushed away Mr Pink-Whistle's hand – and then, because his hand felt so friendly and so kind, he took it after all, and allowed himself to be helped across the road.

'Thanks for helping me,' he said. 'If I could help you in return, maybe I would. But I can't help anyone. I'm just no use at all.'

'You may be sure I'll ask you for help if you can give it,' said Mr Pink-Whistle. 'Goodbye. I'll come and see you again some-time. You live in that small house over there, don't you?'

'Yes,' said the blind man. 'Goodbye.' He went off by himself, tapping with his stick.

Mr Pink-Whistle looked after him. 'It's not fair,' he said. 'Some people have everything – their eyes to see with, good health, friends, love and happiness. And that poor man hasn't anything at all, not even a friend. Yes – it's mostly his own fault, and that only makes it worse!'

The little fat man looked quite sad for once. His eyes lost their twinkle and his mouth drooped. He stood thinking for a moment or two, and then he heard a yelping noise from round the corner. He ran to see what the matter was.

There was a pond round the corner. In it a wet dog struggled for his life. Mr Pink-Whistle waded in and got hold of him. The dog was tied to two big bricks.

'Good gracious!' said Mr Pink-Whistle, cutting the string that bound the dog to the bricks. 'Has someone been trying to drown you?'

'Woof!' said the dog, and as usual Mr Pink-Whistle understood all he said. 'Yes. The old farmer who lives down the hill sent his man to drown me this morning.'

'How dreadful!' cried Mr Pink-Whistle, trying to dry the dog with his handkerchief. 'Why did he want to do that, little dog?'

'Well, you see,' said the dog sadly. 'I'm so ugly. Look at me and see. My head's too big. My tail is too long. My legs are too short. My ears droop down instead of up. And I'm such an ugly red colour. Everyone laughs at me when they see me, and really, I don't wonder. I saw myself once in a looking-glass outside a shop, and I laughed too.'

'It isn't fair,' said Mr Pink-Whistle, patting the dog. 'You've got a good heart, I am sure, and would be a splendid house-dog. That's all that really matters.'

'Oh, I would, I would!' barked the dog, and he licked Mr Pink-Whistle's hand with a long pink tongue. 'Couldn't you have me for your own? All the other puppies went to good homes, but nobody has ever wanted *me.*'

And then Mr Pink-Whistle had a wonderful idea. 'Listen!' he said. 'I know a poor, ugly, blind man, who is lonely and sad. He wants someone to love him and look after him – someone to sit with him in the evenings, and to guide him when he goes

out for walks. He sometimes falls off the
kerb, you know. Now do you think your
heart is large enough to be this poor man's
dog?'

'I would like it better than anything!'
yelped the dog. 'But won't he hate me,
because I'm ugly?'

'He won't be able to see you,' said Mr
Pink-Whistle. 'Come with me now, and we
will see what happens.'

So the still-wet dog and the little fat man
went to the cottage where the blind man
lived. He was there, for he had just come in.

'Hello!' said Mr Pink-Whistle, stepping
into the parlour. 'I'm soon back again – and
to ask your help too! I've got a poor little
dog here, not much more than a puppy, that
someone has tried to drown. Could I dry
him by the fire, do you think?'

'I'll get a towel,' said the blind man, and
he felt his way to a chest, pulled open a drawer and drew out a big brown towel. He went
to the hearthrug and knelt down. 'Where's
the dog?' he said. 'I used to be fond of dogs,
but now even they growl when they see me!'

The wet puppy put out his tongue and
gently licked the blind man on the hand. He

whined a little. The blind man began to dry
him. 'You poor wet creature!' he said. 'So
people are unkind to you too, are they? Well,
there are two of us, then! Are you hungry?
I've got some milk in the larder, and a bone
too, I believe. Hey, you, there – would you
get them?'

He was calling to Mr Pink-Whistle, but will
you believe it, Mr Pink-Whistle didn't answer
a word. No – he just stood by the door, smil-
ing, and the blind man thought he had
gone. Mr Pink-Whistle wanted him to do as

much as possible for the dog, for he knew that was the right way for them to make friends.

So the man fetched the milk and the bone. He found some biscuits too. He sat down by the fire and listened to the dog eating the food.

And then the puppy-dog jumped on to the man's knees, settled himself comfortably there, and licked the man's hands lovingly. Then he pushed his soft head against the man's face and licked his nose.

'Good dog, good fellow!' said the blind man, and he patted the dog. 'You don't mind how ugly and bad-tempered I am, do you? Well – I won't turn you out just yet. You can stay for a while.'

So the dog stayed. He shared the man's tea with him. He found an old ball and rolled it over the floor. The man heard him playing and smiled for the first time for months. 'See you don't leave it for me to fall over,' he said. So the dog rolled it under the couch when he had finished.

'I don't think I can very well turn you out tonight,' said the blind man, when it was bedtime. 'I will keep you tonight, and when the man who brought you comes back, you shall go then.'

The dog went to sleep on the hearthrug. But in the middle of the night he awoke and heard the blind man tossing and turning. He was always loneliest and unhappiest at night. The dog knew this at once, and he ran to the bed. He jumped up on to the eiderdown and snuggled down beside the man, his nose in the man's hand.

'Good fellow!' said the blind man, patting him. 'Good fellow!'

And do you know, when Mr Pink-Whistle came that way again, he saw the puppy-dog gambolling round happily, as fat as butter, and the blind man rolling a ball for him which the dog kept fetching and bringing back.

'Hello!' said Mr Pink-Whistle.

'Hello!' cried the blind man. 'You haven't come to fetch the dog have you? I couldn't do without him. You've no idea what a friend he is to me. He loves me and never leaves me for a minute. He guides me when I go out, and he sleeps on my bed at night. He's the finest dog in the world!'

'And my master's the kindest, best man in the world!' yelped the dog. 'He belongs to me. I look after him and make him happy. He doesn't even know I'm ugly!'

'Good!' said Mr Pink-Whistle, looking at the happy face of the blind man, who was no longer ugly and bad-tempered. 'Very good! A little love and friendship go a very long way! Goodbye!'

Chapter 8

The Forgotten Rabbits

In a nice wooden hutch in a lovely garden lived two rabbits. Their names were Bubble and Squeak, and they were very pretty. Their ears were long and floppy, and their noses went up and down all day long.

They belonged to Winnie and Morris. At first the children had been most excited over their rabbits, and had brought them all kinds of delicious food every hour or two. Then they had grown used to them, and had cleaned their cage out and given them food once a day.

And now, lately, they had begun to forget all about them!

For two whole days the hutch had not been cleaned out! For two whole days the rabbits had had no fresh food.

Mother began to wonder if the rabbits were well looked after, and she went down to see. She was very angry when she found that their cage was so dirty and they had no food at all!

'I shall give the rabbits away,' she told Winnie and Morris. 'If you can't look after your own animals, you are not fit to have any.'

'Oh, don't do that,' said Winnie who really liked her rabbits, though she was lazy and couldn't be bothered to remember them. 'I'll clean out the hutch and feed them, really I will, Mummy.'

But she didn't. She remembered for three days, and then she forgot again. And this time her Mummy was away and didn't see that the rabbits were forgotten! Auntie Jane was there to look after the children, and she quite thought that Winnie and Morris could be trusted to see to Bubble and Squeak.

The rabbits were hungry. They gnawed at their cage and tried to get out. They could see the green grass and they could see the cabbages in the kitchen-garden and the nice juicy lettuces. They felt as if they must get to them, somehow.

So they gnawed and they gnawed with their sharp teeth. And after three days, when they were so hungry that they could almost have eaten the wire netting, Bubble made a hole nearly big enough to squeeze through! But not *quite* big enough.

Poor Bubble! He tried to squash his soft body through the hole – and he stuck! He couldn't get forwards and he couldn't get backwards. It was really dreadful.

He began to squeal, and a rabbit squeal is a noise that makes everyone want to rush to

its help. There was nobody in the house to hear, because the children and their aunt were out – but Mr Pink-Whistle heard.

He was walking at the end of the street, quite a long way away – but he heard the rabbit squealing, for he had ears that heard all cries of sadness and pain. He stopped and listened. He ran back down the road in a hurry, rushed into the front gate, round the house, and down the garden to where the rabbit hutch was.

He soon saw what had happened to poor Bubble! He carefully cut the hole a little wider, took out the frightened rabbit, and placed it back in the hutch.

'Oh, thank you,' said Bubble, who knew at once that the little fat man was half a brownie.

Mr Pink-Whistle looked rather stern. 'You should not have tried to escape,' he said. 'That was a punishment to you, for trying to run away from a good hutch and kind owners.'

'Please, it isn't a good hutch, and Winnie and Morris are not kind,' said Bubble at once. 'Look – did you ever see such a dirty hutch and nasty hay? Can you see any food at all?'

Mr Pink-Whistle looked – and he frowned.

'No,' he said. 'There is no food at all – and the hutch is very dirty. Are Winnie and Morris unkind to you?'

'Oh yes,' said Squeak, her nose twitching hard, up and down, up and down. 'They often forget us. One day we shall die of hunger – and oh, it's dreadful to be hungry and yet see all that food out there, beyond our cage. That's why we tried to escape.'

'You poor, poor things!' said tender-hearted Mr Pink-Whistle. 'Children have no right to keep pets unless they look after them properly! This is a very wicked thing I hear!'

He opened the door of the cage wide. 'Come out, little rabbits,' he said. 'Go and eat all you want – and then run to the hills and live there in a burrow. I will not let these children keep you.'

The rabbits hopped out gladly. They rushed to the lettuces, which grew in the children's own garden, and they ate the whole lot! They ate a row of new green pea-plants, and they nibbled the tops off the young turnips. Oh, they had a wonderful time! Then off they ran to the hills, and found a cosy burrow for the two of them.

Mr Pink-Whistle stared at the empty cage

and his face was sad. 'What a lot of unfair things happen!' he said. 'Those were harmless, kindly little rabbits – and yet Winnie and Morris made them hungry, thin and miserable! Well, I've put things right for Bubble and Squeak – and now I must see to Winnie and Morris!'

He soon saw the children – bonny, fat and healthy, with rosy faces and shining eyes.

'People don't forget *your* meals!' he thought. 'You are chubby and fat. And *your* beds won't be dirty and smelly, unmade for days! No – they will be sweet and clean and fresh! My dear children, I have to teach you a lesson. You won't like it, but I cannot have you treating little creatures, smaller than yourselves, as unkindly as you have treated those two rabbits.'

Mr Pink-Whistle made himself disappear. He couldn't be seen at all. He went into the house and up the stairs, and soon found the children's rooms with their pretty white beds and blue eiderdowns.

Mr Pink-Whistle pulled all the bedclothes off. He jumped on the white sheets with his dirty boots! What a mess he made of those two nice beds!

'Now the children will know what the rabbits felt like, having no nice clean cage to sleep in!' said Mr Pink-Whistle.

He went downstairs. Aunt Jane had placed two plates of delicious-smelling stew on the table for the children who had gone to wash their hands. Mr Pink-Whistle took the plates and emptied them out of the window! Then he put them back on the table.

What a to-do there was when Aunt Jane and the children came into the dining-room!

'How quickly you've eaten your dinner!' cried Aunt Jane.

'We haven't eaten *any* of it!' said Morris, staring in surprise at his empty plate, smeared with gravy.

'You must have,' said Aunt Jane. 'Your plates are empty. Don't tell naughty stories!'

'We're not!' said Winnie. 'Someone's eaten it instead of us. Can we have some more, Aunt Jane?'

'There isn't any,' said her aunt. 'You must have the pudding now. I simply can't understand it!'

Nor could the children. They were hungry and had so much wanted their stew. Aunt Jane went to get the pudding. It was a treacle

pudding, and it sat upright on a big dish.
Just as she set the dish on the table and
turned round to get a spoon, Mr Pink-
Whistle whipped the pudding off the dish
and threw it out of the window!

Plonk! It landed on the grass and broke
into bits. The children screamed in horror.
'Our pudding! It jumped off the dish!'

Aunt Jane hadn't seen what happened.
She was very, very angry. 'You are being
naughty children!' she cried. '*You* threw it
out of the window – I know you did! It must
have been you, for there's no one else here!
Look at it there, smashed on the lawn! Go
up to bed, both of you!'

Crying bitterly the two children went
upstairs to bed – and then they saw their
dirty, untidy beds, with the clothes on the
floor. They called their aunt, and she looked
at the mess in dismay.

'We didn't do it, really we didn't,' sobbed
Winnie. 'Please believe us, Aunt Jane.'

Aunt Jane didn't know what to think. She
made the beds, and told the children to get
undressed. Winnie went to a drawer of
her chest as soon as her aunt had gone. 'I've
got some biscuits and chocolate here,

Morris,' she said. 'Let's have them. I'm so hungry!'

But as soon as she opened her drawer, Mr Pink-Whistle's invisible hand went in, and he took out the packet of biscuits and the bar of chocolate. He threw them out of the window.

The children screamed with rage and fright. Whatever could be happening! Then Mr Pink-Whistle pulled their beds to pieces again and jumped on the sheets!

'Who is it? Who is it? It's someone we can't see!' wept Winnie.

'Yes,' said Mr Pink-Whistle. 'But now you *shall* see me!' He muttered some very magic words – and hey presto! there he was, standing in front of the children, a little fat man with pointed brownie ears and large green eyes.

'Good morning!' he said. 'I'm sorry to behave like this – but for the sake of Bubble and Squeak I have to put things right. You forgot to clean their bed – so I've made your beds dirty and untidy to show you how horrid it is. You forgot to give them food and they went hungry. So I've taken away your food to show you what it's like to be really hungry. What do you think about it?'

'I'm ashamed,' said Winnie, and she hung her head.

'I'm sorry about it,' said Morris, and he went red. 'I'll go straight down to the hutch now and give the rabbits a good feed.'

Off went the children – and found the hutch empty. How they cried!

'It's a hard lesson,' said Mr Pink-Whistle, feeling sad. 'But learn it, my dears, and you'll be happier in the future – and so will your pets. Goodbye!'

He disappeared. Where had he gone? The children couldn't imagine!

Chapter 9

Jimmy's Day in the Country

It was going to be a very exciting day for fifty of the town children. They were all to go for a day in the country. How lovely!

At ten o'clock a big red bus stood waiting at the corner of the road, and the fifty children climbed in with two grown-ups to look after them. Off they went, singing and laughing.

Each child had his lunch with him and his tea, in school-bags. Jimmy had egg sandwiches, two slices of cake, and and an apple for his lunch; and jam sandwiches, two buns, and a piece of chocolate for his tea. He thought it was lovely.

'Now, listen,' said Miss White, one of the grown-ups, when at last the bus arrived at a

farm in the country. 'You may all wander off as you please, and see all the animals on the farm – but be sure not to go out of reach of the bell, because the bus will take us back at five o'clock, and you must all be here then. I shall ring the bell at half-past four to warn you.'

The children ran off, talking happily. Some went to see the pretty new calves. Some ran to see the ducks and the hens. Others begged for a ride on the old brown horse, and Jimmy waited for his turn too. He had been in the country before and he loved it.

Very soon he felt hungry, and he found a sunny place beneath a hedge and sat down to eat his lunch. Oooh! How good the egg sandwiches were! The cake was delicious, and the apple was as sweet as sugar.

'I mustn't eat my tea as well now, though I'd very much like to!' said Jimmy, looking at his jam sandwiches. 'No – I'll leave them till four o'clock.'

He packed up his bag again, put it over his shoulder, and went off across the fields to see if he could find some flowers to take home to his mother.

He knew his way about very well, for he had been down to the farm before. He jumped over a little stream, crossed two fields, and went into a wood. Big pink flowers were growing there, and Jimmy began to make a bunch of them. He went right through the wood, and came out at the other side. There was a field that used to have goats in.

'I wonder if the goats have any babies,' thought Jimmy to himself. 'I love little kidgoats!'

He went to see – and there, under the hedge, he saw a small girl, with tears rolling down her cheeks. She belonged to Jimmy's party, and he looked at her in surprise.

'Whatever's the matter?' he asked.

'It's those horrid goats,' sobbed the small girl, whose name was Margery. 'I came here, and lay down in the sunshine, and somehow I fell asleep. And two big goats came whilst I was asleep and ate all my lunch – yes, and my tea too. And they even ate my bag as well! This is all that's left of it – look!'

She showed him the strap. Jimmy was sorry for her. 'It must be dreadful to have your lunch and your tea both eaten by goats,' he thought.

'Have you eaten your lunch?' asked Margery, looking at his bag hungrily. 'I suppose you couldn't share it with me?'

'I've eaten it,' said Jimmy. And then, because he was a kind boy, he said, 'But you can have my tea if you like! My mother will give me some more when I get home!'

'Oh, thank you!' said Margery – and she ate up every scrap of Jimmy's nice tea – chocolate and all!

'Now I'll take you where there are wild strawberries,' she said. 'I found them last year in the wood.'

But although they hunted for ages and ages they couldn't find any at all. 'It's time for the bell soon, I should think,' said Jimmy. 'Don't let's go too far.'

When the bell rang at half-past four, Jimmy was dreadfully hungry – but his tea was inside Margery! So he couldn't have any! 'Come along,' he said. 'We must go back. The bus will be there.'

So back they went – but Margery was tired and couldn't hurry. And then she fell down and hurt her knee so badly that she howled and howled! Jimmy bathed her knee in some water and tied it up with his handkerchief. Then he tried to hurry Margery along, but she could only limp very slowly, for her knee hurt her.

'We shall miss the bus!' cried Jimmy in despair. 'Do hurry!'

Margery cried. She fell over again. Jimmy knelt down and made her get on his back. 'I'll give you a piggyback,' he said. 'Maybe we'll be quicker then.'

But Margery was heavy and he couldn't carry her for long. 'Let's sit down here and wait for the bus to go by,' said Margery at last. 'We can stop it then.'

So they sat down – but, alas, for them! the bus went another way, and they saw it turning a corner far down the hill, full of children going home!

'Oh, it's too bad!' cried Jimmy, almost in tears. 'I've helped you all I could, Margery, and given you my tea and carried you – and now we've missed the bus and my mother will be worried.'

'Look – here's someone coming,' said Margery. They looked down the lane, and saw a fat little man. It was Mr Pink-Whistle, of course, and he was going home for a little holiday. He had been away from his cottage and his cat, Sooty, for quite a long while.

He saw the children and stopped. 'What's the matter?' he asked.

Margery told him all their story. 'It's too bad for poor Jimmy,' she said. 'He did help me such a lot, and he was so kind – and now I've made him miss the bus and we haven't any money and we've got to walk home, and my knee hurts, and . . .'

'Good gracious me!' said Mr Pink-Whistle. 'How very lucky that I happened to walk down this way. I'll soon put things right! That's what I'm made for, I think – to put things right. But you wouldn't believe what a lot of things go wrong! I'm always hard at work, every single day.'

'I like you,' said Margery, and she put her small hand into Mr Pink-Whistle's rather large one. 'You look a bit like a brownie in my picture book at home. But how can you put things right for us? There isn't another bus home.'

'Oh yes, there is,' said Mr Pink-Whistle. 'It's not the usual bus, you know – it's one that nobody sees but the little folk of the woods! But if you'd really like to see it, just put on these glasses, will you? They will help you.'

He handed the two surprised children a pair of glasses each. They set them on their noses and looked through them.

My goodness! What a marvellous surprise! They could see small brownies peeping at them from the hedge. They could see tiny folk of all sorts running here and there, no bigger than flowers. And they could see a strange little cottage standing not far off, which they were quite certain hadn't been there before!

'It *was* there before,' said Mr Pink-Whistle, 'but you hadn't got those magic glasses on, so you just didn't see it! A friend of mine lives there. Let's see if she will give us tea.'

They went up to the little green door. Rat-tat! The door opened and a small woman stood there, with big pointed ears just like Mr Pink-Whistle's. Her eyes were green too, like his. She beamed all over her face and cried, 'Mr Pink-Whistle! What a lovely surprise! You're just in time for tea. Do come in!'

So they all went in, and Mr Pink-Whistle told his friend, Dame Little, all about Jimmy and Margery. They sat down to tea – and, my goodness, what a tea it was! There were wild strawberries and cream. There were little biscuits shaped like flowers. There were cakes shaped like animals, and they were full of cream. The funny part about them was that when you pressed them, each cake squeaked! But Jimmy didn't squeeze too hard, because it shot the cream out! What a tea it was!

'The bus will be by soon,' said Dame Little. So they shook hands with her, and she took them to her gate. Down the lane came

the bus – but what a bus! It was shaped like a Noah's ark on wheels, and you had to climb up a ladder and get in at the lid, which the conductor held open!

Inside there were rows of seats, and on them sat rabbits, moles, a hedgehog, brownies, and many other passengers. They looked rather surprised to see the children, but made room for them most politely. The strange bus started off and the conductor shut the lid.

'This is a most surprising adventure,' said Jimmy. 'I can't believe it's true.'

'Well, you don't need to believe, it,' said Mr Pink-Whistle, laughing. 'Think it's a dream, if you like – it will be just as exciting, either way!'

The bus stopped at the end of the children's street, and they got out, yawning. 'Thank you very much, Mr Pink-Whistle,' began Jimmy, but Mr Pink-Whistle was gone – and so was the bus.

'*Was* it a dream, do you think?' said Margery to Jimmy. 'I wish I knew!'

'Well, all I can say is that I'm jolly glad I helped you, Margery,' said Jimmy. 'I'd never have had this lovely adventure if I hadn't!'

Chapter 10

The Mean Little Boy

There was once a mean little boy called Wilfrid. He took other children's toys away and wouldn't give them back. He pinched the little girls when no grown-up was about. He hit the little boys, and sometimes threw their caps right up into the trees so that they couldn't get them.

Wilfrid was big and rather strong for his age, and it wasn't much good trying to stop him. All that the other children could do was to run away when they saw him.

But one day little Janet didn't run away quickly enough. She was playing with her tricycle in the street and Wilfrid saw her. He loved riding on tricycles because he hadn't got one himself – so up he ran and caught hold of the handle.

'Get off, Janet. I want a ride,' said Wilfrid.

'No,' said Janet. 'You are much bigger than I am, and my mother says I mustn't let bigger children ride my little tricycle in case they break it.'

'Well, I'm jolly well going to ride it!' said Wilfrid. He dragged Janet off her tricycle and she fell on the ground. Wilfrid was always so rough. Then he got on the little tricycle himself and rode off quickly down the street, ringing the bell loudly.

My word, how quickly he went! You should have seen him. All the other children skipped out of the way, and even the grown-ups did, too. Ting-a-ling-a-ling! went the bell – ting-a-ling-a-ling!

Wilfrid came to where the street began to go down a little hill. On he went, just as fast – and then he came to a roadway. He tried to stop, but he couldn't. Over the kerb he went, crash! The tricycle fell over, and Wilfrid fell too.

He didn't hurt himself – but the tricycle was quite broken! The handle was off, the bell was spoilt and wouldn't ring, and one of the pedals was broken!

A little fat man with pointed ears and green eyes saw the accident. It was Mr Pink-Whistle of course, trotting along as usual to see what bad things in the world he could put right.

He hurried up to the boy who had fallen, meaning to pick him up and comfort him, but before he could get there a little girl ran up and began to scold him, crying bitterly all the time.

'You horrid boy, Wilfrid! Now you've broken my tricycle and I did love it so much.

My mother will be very angry with me because you rode it. I shan't be able to get it mended, and it will have to be put away in the shed and never ridden any more!'

And Janet cried bucketfuls of tears all down herself till her dress was quite damp. The other children came running up to see what had happened. They glared at Wilfrid, who made a face and slapped Janet because she cried so loudly.

'It's a silly tricycle anyway!' said Wilfrid. 'Stupid baby one. Good gracious, I might have broken my leg, falling over like that!'

He stalked off, whistling, leaving the others to pick up the tricycle and to comfort poor Janet.

'Horrid boy!' said Tom. 'Don't cry, Janet.'

'Yes, but it isn't fair!' wept Janet. 'It's *my* tricycle, and he took it away from me – and now it's broken and my mother will be so cross.'

Mr Pink-Whistle was sorry for the little girl. He walked up to the children and patted Janet's golden head.

'Now, now, don't cry any more,' he said. 'Maybe *I* can mend your tricycle. Tell me some more about the boy who broke it.'

Well, you should have heard the things that came pouring out about Wilfrid, the mean boy! Mr Pink-Whistle didn't care whether it was telling tales or not – he just *had* to know about him. And soon he knew so much that a big frown came above his green eyes and he pursed up his pink mouth.

'Hmmmm,' said Mr Pink-Whistle, deep down in his throat. 'I must see into this. That boy wants punishing. But first we will mend your tricycle, little girl.'

Well, Mr Pink-Whistle took the broken tricycle along to a bicycle shop, and soon it was as good as new. The handle was put on again very firmly. A new bell was bought and fixed on. It was much better than the other one. The pedal was nicely mended – and then Janet got on her tricycle and rode off in delight.

'Oh, thank you!' she cried. 'But I do hope I don't meet Wilfrid! He will want to ride my tricycle again and break it!'

'I'll look after Wilfrid!' said Mr Pink-Whistle. And then, in his very sudden and extraordinary way, he disappeared! One minute he was there – and the next he wasn't. But really and truly he *was* there –

but quite invisible, because, as you know, he was half magic.

He had seen Wilfrid coming along again – and Mr Pink-Whistle meant to watch that small boy and see all the things he did! Yes – Wilfrid wasn't going to have a very good time now.

Wilfrid strolled along, hands in pockets, making faces at children he met. When he met Kenneth, who was eating a rosy apple, Wilfrid stopped.

'Give me that apple!' he said.

'No!' said Kenneth, putting the apple behind his back. Wilfrid snatched at it – and it rolled into the mud so that nobody could eat it at all!

Kenneth yelled. Wilfrid grinned. Mr Pink-Whistle frowned. The little fat man bought another apple at the fruit-shop and slipped it into Kenneth's pocket without being seen. He would find it there when he got home – what a lovely surprise!

Then Mr Pink-Whistle suddenly became visible again, and walked into a shop. He bought several rather large sheets of white paper, some pins, and some black chalk. He stood by a wall and quickly wrote something in big letters on a sheet of paper.

Then he disappeared suddenly – but a very strange thing happened. On Wilfrid's back a large sheet of white paper suddenly appeared, and was gently pinned there so that Wilfrid didn't know. On the paper was written a single sentence in big black letters: 'I KNOCKED KENNETH'S APPLE INTO THE MUD!'

Well, Wilfrid went along the street humming gaily, not knowing that anything was on his back at all. But very soon all the children knew it. First one saw it, then another – and soon a big crowd was following Wilfrid, giggling hard.

Wilfrid heard them and turned round.

'What's the joke?' he asked.

'*You're* the joke!' said Harry.

'You stop giggling and tell me *how* I'm the joke!' said Wilfrid fiercely.

'Who knocked Kenneth's apple into the mud?' called Jenny.

'How do you know I did?' cried Wilfrid. 'I suppose that baby Kenneth has been telling tales. Wait till I see him again!'

'No he hasn't told us – you told us yourself, giggled Doris.

'I didn't,' said Wilfrid.

'Look on your back!' shouted Lennie.

Wilfrid screwed his head and looked over his shoulder. He caught sight of something white on his back. He dragged at his coat and pulled off the paper. He read it and went red with rage.

'Who dared to pin this on my back!' he shouted. 'I'll shake him till his teeth rattle!'

Everyone shook their heads. No – they hadn't pinned the paper on Wilfrid's back, though they would have liked to, if they had dared.

Wilfrid threw the paper on to the ground and stamped on it. 'If anyone does that to me again, they'll be sorry for themselves!' he said fiercely. 'So just look out!'

But the one who had done it didn't care a rap for Wilfrid's threat. No – old Pink-Whistle grinned to himself and trotted quietly along after Wilfrid, waiting to see what mean thing the boy would do next.

And then out would come another sheet of paper, of course – and Wilfrid would have to wear another notice on his back.

Chapter 11

Wilfrid Has a
Good Many Shocks

Mr Pink-Whistle followed Wilfrid home, and then he sat on the wall outside, still invisible, to wait for him to come out. Inside the house he could hear Wilfrid being very rude to his mother.

'Wilfrid, I want you to run down and get me some potatoes,' said his mother.

'I don't want to, I'm tired,' said the selfish boy.

'Now you do as you're told, Wilfrid,' said his mother. 'Hurry up.'

'Shan't!' said Wilfrid. 'I'm tired, I tell you.'

Mr Pink-Whistle listened, quite horrified. To think that any boy could talk to his mother like that! It was simply dreadful. Wilfrid went on being rude – and then, when his mother had gone to the back door to speak to the baker, Wilfrid slipped out of the front door. *He* wasn't going to go and fetch potatoes, not he!

Mr Pink-Whistle had been busy writing something on a sheet of white paper with his black chalk. He waited till Wilfrid passed him, and then the little fat man neatly pinned the paper on to Wilfrid's back. He did it with such a magic touch that the boy didn't feel anything at all. Off went Wilfrid down the street, whistling – and on his back the sheet of paper said: 'I HAVE BEEN VERY RUDE TO MY MOTHER!'

Well, it wasn't long before all the passers-by saw the paper and began to laugh at it. 'Fancy!' they said to one another, 'he has been rude to his mother! Well, he certainly looks a most unpleasant boy, it's true – but fancy being rude to his *mother*!'

The other children soon saw the notice and gathered round, giggling. Wilfrid glared at them. Whatever was all the giggling about?

'You've been rude to your mother!' shouted Kenneth.

'Bad boy! You've been rude to your mother!' yelled all the children.

Wilfrid stopped in surprise. Now how in the world did the others know that? He hadn't told anyone – and his mother certainly hadn't, for she would be too much ashamed of her son to say such a thing.

'How do you know?' he demanded angrily.

'You've got it on your back,' shouted the children in glee.

Wilfrid tore the paper off his back and looked at it. How he scowled when he saw what was printed there! But how could it have got on his back? And who could have written that sentence?

He tore the paper into little pieces and stuffed them into a litter bin. Then he stamped off angrily. Just wait till he caught anyone pinning paper on his back again! He kept turning round quickly to make sure that no one was creeping behind him.

Soon he met Alison, and she had a bag of sweets. 'Give me one!' said Wilfrid.

'No,' said Alison bravely. Wilfrid gave her such a pinch that she squealed loudly and ran away, hugging her bag of sweets and crying.

Well, you can guess that it wasn't more than half a minute before Mr Pink-Whistle had pinned another sheet of paper on

Wilfrid's back! This time it said, in bold black letters: 'I HAVE PINCHED ALISON AND MADE HER CRY.'

Everyone who saw it looked surprised – and then grinned. 'What a nasty little boy that must be!' they thought. They wondered if he knew that he had the paper on his back. He didn't know at first – but as soon as he met some other children, he knew at once!

For they danced around him, shouting, 'You pinched Alison! You horrid boy! You pinched Alison and made her cry!'

'How do you know?' shouted Wilfrid. 'Did she tell tales of me?'

'No – you're telling tales about yourself!' yelled back the children, keeping a good distance away from the angry little boy. He at once felt round at his back and tore off the paper. When he read what was written he was rather frightened. He felt quite certain that no one had been near enough to him to pin on that paper – he had been keeping a good watch. Then how did it get on his back?

Wilfrid thought he would go home. He didn't like these strange happenings at all. It wasn't a bit funny suddenly to have horrid things pinned on his back for people to laugh at. He ran home quickly.

His mother was out in the garden. Wilfrid thought that no one else was in the house, so he crept to the jam cupboard, and looked for a pot of strawberry jam. He didn't know that Mr Pink-Whistle was just behind him, quite invisible! The naughty boy ran off with the jam and sat down under a bush in the front garden to enjoy it.

Mr Pink-Whistle busily wrote on another sheet of paper, then sat down beside Wilfrid,

and pinned it gently on his back. The boy couldn't see Mr Pink-Whistle, of course, and he was so busy with the jam that he didn't even hear the very slight rustle of the paper.

He finished the jam and went indoors, and as soon as he turned round his mother saw what was pinned on his back: 'I HAVE STOLEN A POT OF STRAWBERRY JAM.'

'Oh, *have* you!' said Wilfrid's mother, and she went to her jam cupboard to look. Sure enough a pot was gone.

'Wilfrid! You bad boy! You've taken my jam!' she cried. 'Go straight upstairs to bed and stay there for the rest of the day! Go quickly before I scold you some more!'

Wilfrid rushed upstairs, for his mother was really very angry indeed. He took his coat off to undress – and saw the notice that said so plainly, 'I HAVE STOLEN A POT OF STRAWBERRY JAM.'

Wilfrid stared at it, frightened. Who had seen him take the jam? Who had pinned that notice on him? It was magic. It couldn't be anything else. Wilfrid began to cry.

'Oh, it's all very well to cry,' said the voice of Mr Pink-Whistle in the bedroom. 'You cry just because you are frightened – not because you are sorry. You are a very horrid, rude and mean little boy.'

'Oh, who's speaking to me?' asked Wilfrid, staring all round the room and seeing nobody. 'I'm so frightened. Please, please, don't pin any more notices on me. I can't bear it.'

'I shall go on pinning notices on you just as long as you do things that deserve it,' said Mr Pink-Whistle. 'I say again – you are a very horrid, rude and mean little boy.'

There was a silence. Mr Pink-Whistle had gone. Wilfrid slowly got undressed and climbed into bed. He lay there with nothing to do, thinking very hard.

Yes – the strange voice was right. He was a horrid boy. He had spoilt Kenneth's apple – broken Janet's tricycle – been rude to his mother – stolen her pot of jam – pinched Alison – good gracious, what a long list of horridness!

'If only I could put things right!' thought Wilfrid uncomfortably. 'It's so easy to do something wrong – and so difficult to put it right afterwards.'

His mother came into the room, very angry. Wilfrid called to her, 'Mother! I'm sorry I was rude today – and please forgive me for taking the jam. I never will again. Can I take some money out of my money-box and buy another pot for you?'

'Well – that would be very nice of you and would put everything right again, Wilfrid,' said his mother, surprised and pleased. 'You can get up and go and buy it now, before you change your mind.'

'I shan't change my mind,' said Wilfrid, and he hurriedly dressed again. He had been saving up to buy a big bow and some arrows – but never mind! He tipped all the money out of his box. There was eight pounds and thirty pence. He put it all into his pocket.

He rushed out. He went to the grocer's and bought a large pot of best strawberry jam. He went to the greengrocer's and bought two apples for Kenneth. He went to the toy shop and bought a doll for Alison, and a tricycle basket for Janet. All his money was spent!

The other children were most astonished when they saw Wilfrid coming along looking ashamed and shy! He was always so bold and rude!

'Kenneth – here's something for you,' said Wilfrid, and he pushed the apples into the boy's hands. 'Alison – I didn't mean to hurt you and make you cry. Here's a doll to make up for it. And, Janet – here's a new basket to put on the front of your tricycle. I'm sorry I broke it.'

'Oh, Wilfrid!' cried all three children in the greatest delight. 'How nice of you! Thank you very much.'

Wilfrid went red and ran home with the jam. He gave it to his mother and she kissed him.

'There's nobody can be nicer than you when you really try!' she said.

'Really, Mother?' said Wilfrid, feeling very happy all of a sudden. 'Oh, Mother – I don't know how those horrid notices came on my back, but I do hope there won't be any more, now I've tried to put things right!'

Well – there was one more! Mr Pink-Whistle had watched Wilfrid trying to put things right, and he was pleased. He followed the boy about for a few more days and saw that he really was trying to be better. So he put one more notice on Wilfrid's back – and then went off to another town to see if he could find something else to put right.

What was on that last paper? Something that Wilfrid didn't mind at all! It said: 'I REALLY HAVE BEEN DOING MY BEST!'

And all the children clapped their hands and cried, 'Yes, Wilfrid – you have!"

Enid Blyton titles available at Bloomsbury
Children's Books

Adventure!
Mischief at St Rollo's
The Children of Kidillin
The Secret of Cliff Castle
Smuggler Ben
The Boy Who Wanted a Dog
The Adventure of the Secret Necklace

Happy Days!
Run-About's Holiday
Bimbo and Topsy
Hello Mr Twiddle
Shuffle the Shoemaker
Mr Meddle's Mischief
Snowball the Pony
The Adventures of Binkle and Flip

Enid Blyton Age-Ranged Story Collections
Best Stories for Five-Year-Olds
Best Stories for Six-Year-Olds
Best Stories for Seven-Year-Olds
Best Stories for Eight-Year-Olds